Dear Parent:
Your child's love of reading starts here!

Every child learns to read in a different way and at his or her own speed. Some go back and forth between reading levels and read favourite books again and again. Others read through each level in order. You can help your young reader improve and become more confident by encouraging his or her own interests and abilities. From books your child reads with you to the first books he or she reads alone, there are I Can Read Books for every stage of reading:

SHARED READING
Basic language, word repetition, and whimsical illustrations, ideal for sharing with your emergent reader

BEGINNING READING
Short sentences, familiar words, and simple concepts for children eager to read on their own

READING WITH HELP
Engaging stories, longer sentences, and language play for developing readers

READING ALONE
Complex plots, challenging vocabulary, and high-interest topics for the independent reader

ADVANCED READING
Short paragraphs, chapters, and exciting themes for the perfect bridge to chapter books

I Can Read Books have introduced children to the joy of reading since 1957. Featuring award-winning authors and illustrators and a fabulous cast of beloved characters, I Can Read Books set the standard for beginning readers.

A lifetime of discovery begins with the magical words **"I Can Read!"**

Visit www.icanread.com
on enriching your child's r

First published in the UK by HarperCollins Children's Books in 2008
HarperCollins Children's Books is a division of HarperCollins Publishers Ltd.

1 3 5 7 9 10 8 6 4 2

ISBN-13: 978-0-00-727680-6
ISBN-10: 0-00-727680-X

Printed and bound in China

INDIANA JONES

and the

KINGDOM OF THE CRYSTAL SKULL

MEET MUTT

HarperCollins *Children's Books*

Meet Mutt Williams.

He always wears jeans
and a leather jacket.

Sometimes Mutt

can be a bit of a rebel.

Everywhere he goes
Mutt loves to ride
his motorcycle.

You might be surprised
to learn that Mutt is a
champion fencing star.

His school skills are helpful
when he's on adventures with Indy.

Sometimes even a rebel like Mutt
has to admit he needs a little help.

Mutt meets Professor Jones
at Marshall College.
He has a letter to decipher.

Mutt's mother and her friend, Oxley, were kidnapped while looking for a mysterious crystal skull.
Only their old friend, Indy, can save them now.

Indy reads the letter –
Mutt's mother is in danger!
They head off to South America
right away to help her.
But they have people
chasing them, too.

Mutt and Indy make a pretty good team.
They can certainly handle themselves
in a fight.

Indy and Mutt find
the crystal skull
in a cemetery in Peru.
Mutt thinks it's weird.

Mutt needs Indy's help
to get out of a few scrapes,
such as escaping the bad guys
and giant ants.

Sometimes Mutt
is the one helping Indy!
Did someone say
he doesn't like snakes?

At last Indy helps Mutt find his mother –
who turns out to be Marion Ravenwood,
an old flame of Indy's!

Though Indy and Mutt have found
Marion and Oxley,
their adventures are just starting!

JOIN THE QUEST FOR THE CRYSTAL SKULL WITH ALL THESE COOL INDIANA JONES BOOKS

Meet Indy:
I Can Read

Meet Mutt:
I Can Read

Indiana Jones and the Kingdom of the Crystal Skull movie novel

Indiana Jones and the Kingdom of the Crystal Skull movie storybook

Indiana Jones and the Kingdom of the Crystal Skull activity book with tattoos